This Little Tiger book belongs to:

For Nuria ~ P. B.

To Dennis, thanks for Wednesdays ~ M. T.

LITTLE TIGER PRESS LTD,
an imprint of the Little Tiger Group · 1 Coda Studios, 189 Munster Road, London SW6 6AW
Imported into the EEA by Penguin Random House Ireland, Morrison Chambers, 32 Nassau Street, Dublin D02 YH68
www.littletiger.co.uk
First published in Great Britain 2010
This edition published 2017

A CIP catalogue record for this book is available from the British Library ·
ISBN 978-1-84869-798-0 · Printed in China · LTP/2700/4259/0122
10 9 8 7 6 5

WHAT'S MORE SCARY THAN A SHARK?

by Paul Bright

Illustrated by Michael Terry

LITTLE TIGER

LONDON

Shark was SERIOUSLY SCARY. His eyes were dark and SCARY. His smile was cold and SCARY, and his teeth were very, very sharp . . . and SCARY.

If a young fish ever asked his mother, "What is the SCARIEST thing in the sea?" the answer was always the same: SCARY SHARK!

Only Lobster wasn't scared of Shark. He was far too hard and tough to be a tasty meal.

"**YOU GREAT TOOTHY-JAWS!**" said Lobster. "Leave us alone and pick on someone your own size."

And someone Shark's own size was coming. As BIG as Shark, as SCARY as Shark. It was another shark, and her name was **Sadie**.

Shark stared at **Sadie**.

His scary eyes went wibbly,

his scary smile went wobbly,

and his sharp, scary teeth went

chitter-chitter-chatter.

"Lobster," said Shark. "Help me. I don't know what to do.

I've gone all **floppity!** I'm in . . . **LOVE!**"

"Well, what a **SOPPY-SOCKS** you are," said Lobster. "Give her a present. Something girly, like . . . a bunch of seaweed."

"Just **ONE** bunch?" said Shark. "I'll give her **ALL** the seaweed in the sea. But if she doesn't like it, goggle-eyes, I'll scrunch your crunchy shell and use your claws for toothpicks!"

Shark raced here and there.
He found green seaweed,
red seaweed, thin and
stringy seaweed, flat and
flapping seaweed.

He arranged it all into a big, big
bunch, then swam nervously
towards **Sadie**.

But the bunch of seaweed was SO BIG, he couldn't see anything. He bashed into a rock with a

CRASH!

and **Sadie** didn't notice him at all.

"The seaweed didn't work," said Shark, frantically. "What do I do **NOW?**"

Lobster thought hard. "What you need, **BARNACLE-BRAIN**, is a pearl," he said. "Find her a big, sparkly pearl!"

"Big? Sparkly?" said Shark. "I'll give her the BIGGEST, SPARKLIEST pearl in the whole ocean! But if she doesn't like it, clunky-claws, it's lobster and seaweed salad for dinner!"

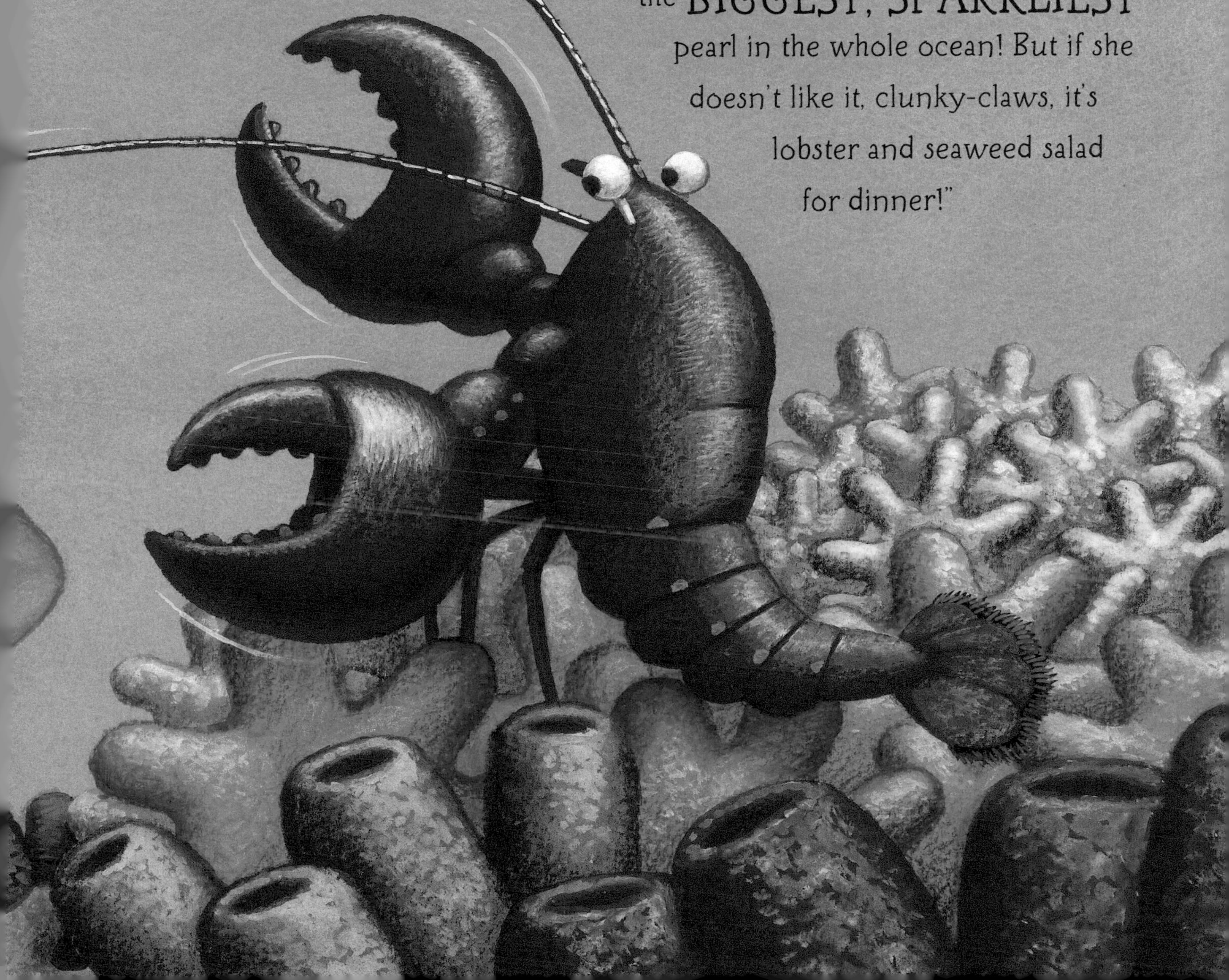

Shark searched until he found the BIGGEST oyster, with the BIGGEST, SPARKLIEST pearl in the whole ocean. Shark asked for the pearl as politely as a shark can: "Give me your pearl or I'll SQUASH you!"

"No!" said the oyster. "It's mine!"

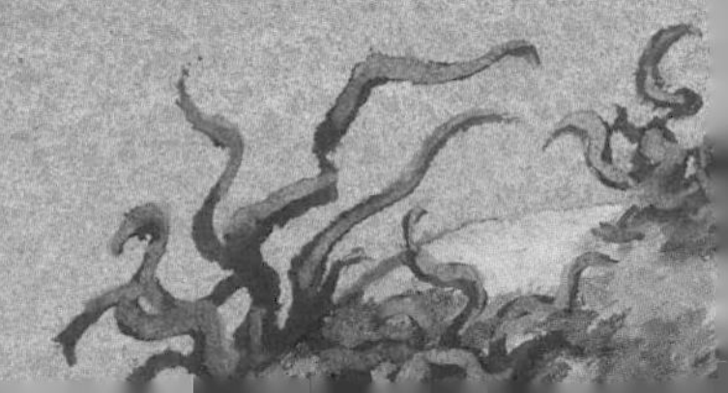

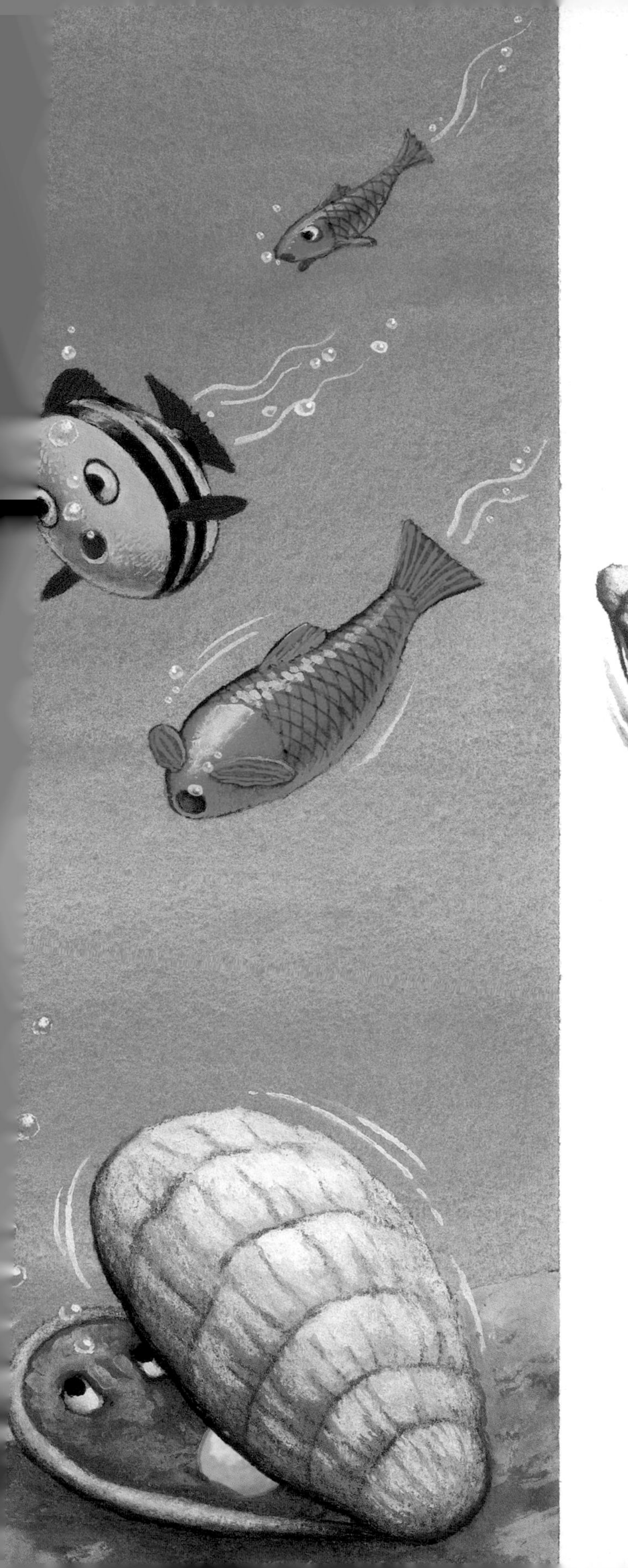

So Shark reached in to grab the pearl with his teeth. But the oyster shut her shell with a

SNAP!

right on his nose.

"The pearl BIT me!" said Shark. "There MUST be something else Sadie will like! Something that doesn't BITE!"

"Don't panic, SNAPPY-SNOUT," said Lobster. "Sing her a love song! I know a choir of angelfish who can join in and go 'boop-boop-de-doop!' and make it really sweet."

"That's it! The BEST idea yet!" said Shark.

Shark started to do some singing exercises:

"LA LA LA LA LAAA!"

he sang, very loudly.

"LO LO LO LO LOOO!"

he sang, very softly.

Lobster hurried off, then came back with the angelfish. They were very scared of Shark, but did as they were told and swam into position near to **Sadie**.

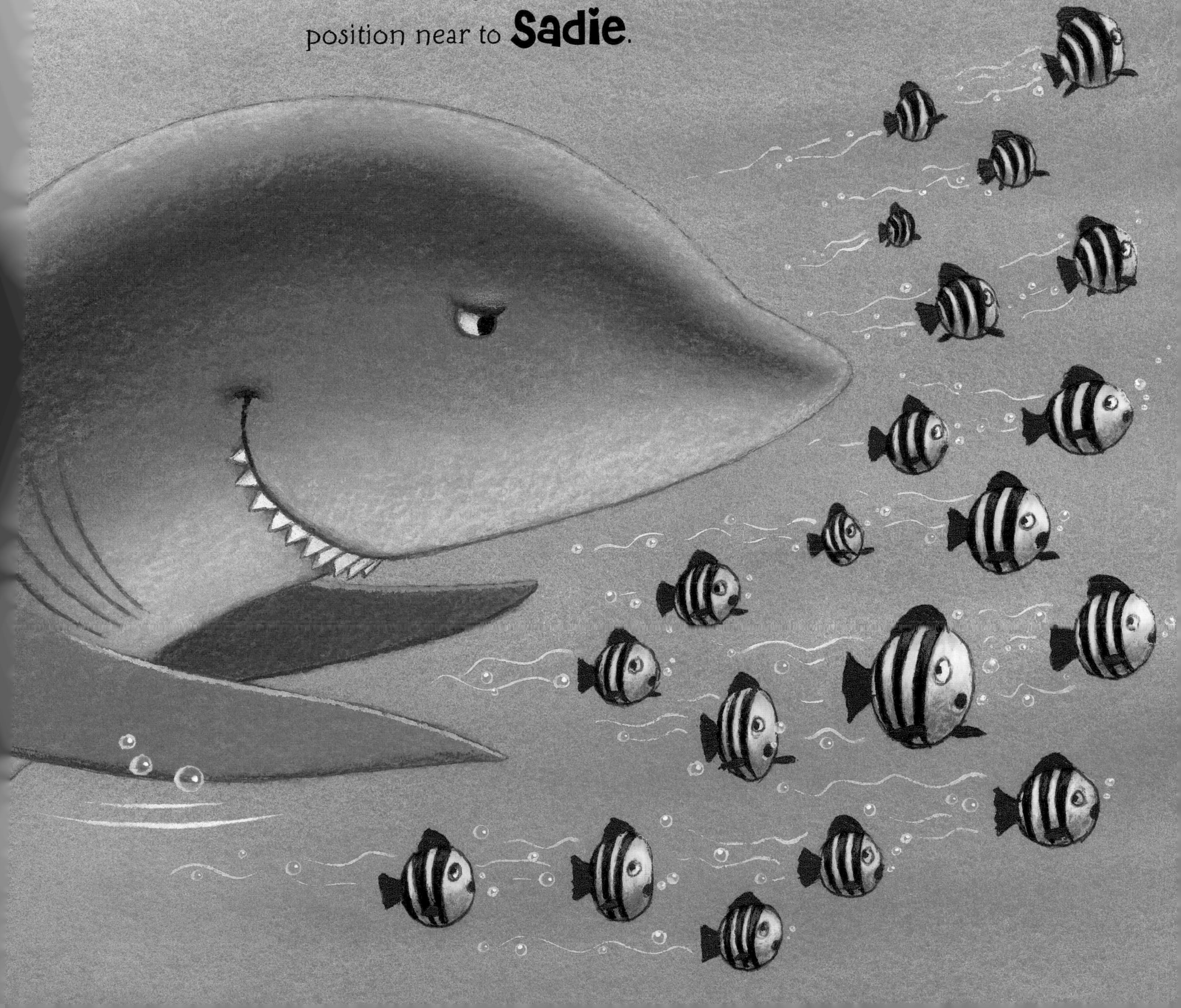

Shark started to sing: "You make
my heart go bibbly-bobbly!"
And the angelfish joined
in, so, so sweetly:
"Boop-boop-de-doop!"

"You make my

heart go bibbly-bobbly!"

Boop-boop-de-doop!
Boop-boop-de-doop!
Boop-boop-de-doop!
Boop-boop-de-doop!
Boop-boop-de-doop!

Then at last **Sadie** turned, and smiled.
Shark gasped with joy, and felt his heart
going more bibbly-bobbly than ever.
He sang again: "You make my fins go
wibbly-wobbly!" And to his delight,
Sadie swam closer and closer and . . .

CHOMP!

. . the angelfish were GONE!

"BRISTLING BARNACLES!"

exclaimed Lobster.

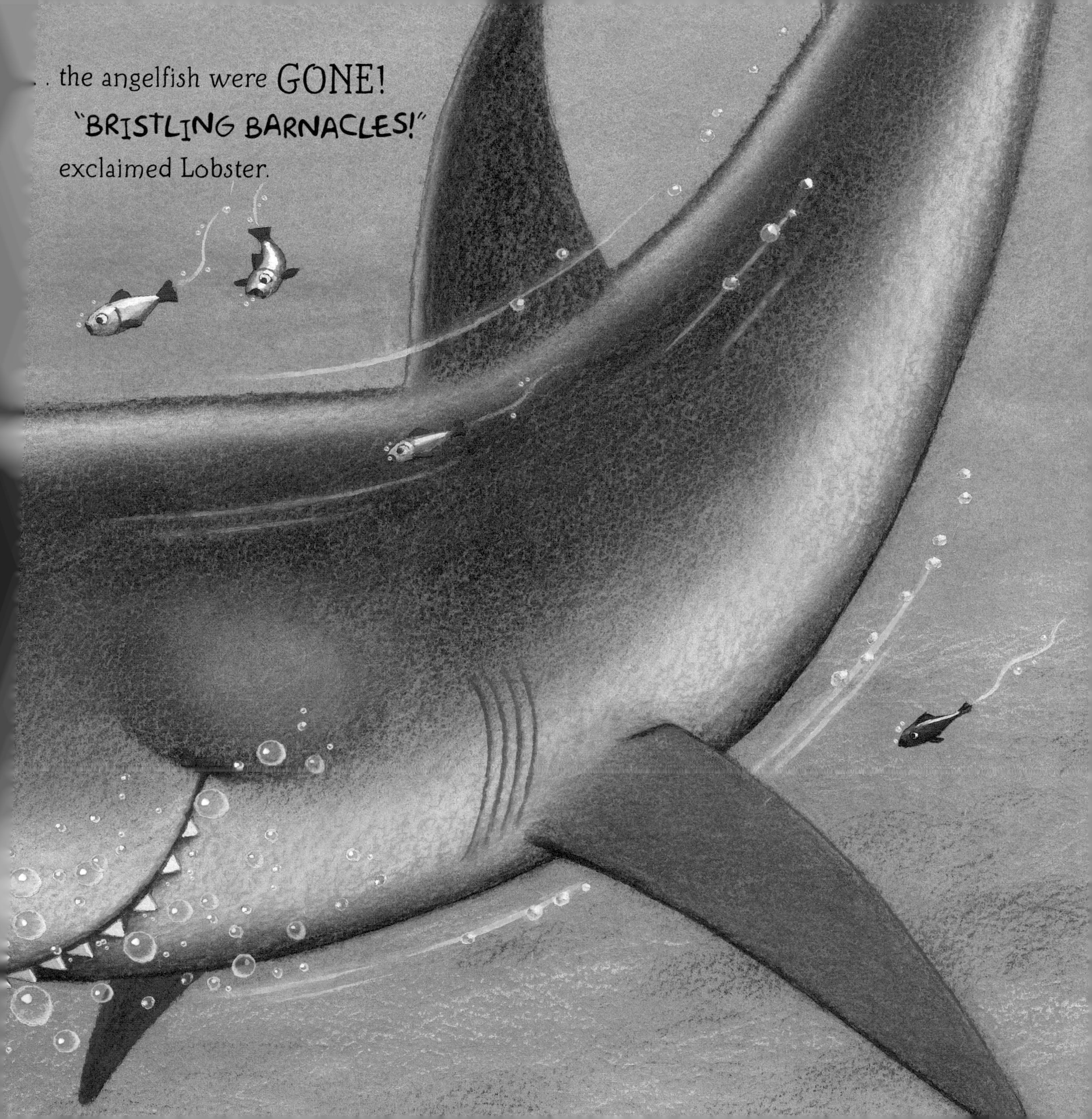

"What a lovely present," said **Sadie**. "They were delicious!"

"Wow!" said Shark. "You are the **SCARIEST**!

Will you be my own **SCARY SWEETHEART**?"

"I will," said **Sadie**.

They touched noses, and Shark's heart went all **bibbly-bibbly-bobbly**, and **Sadie's** fins went all **wibbly-wibbly-wobbly**.

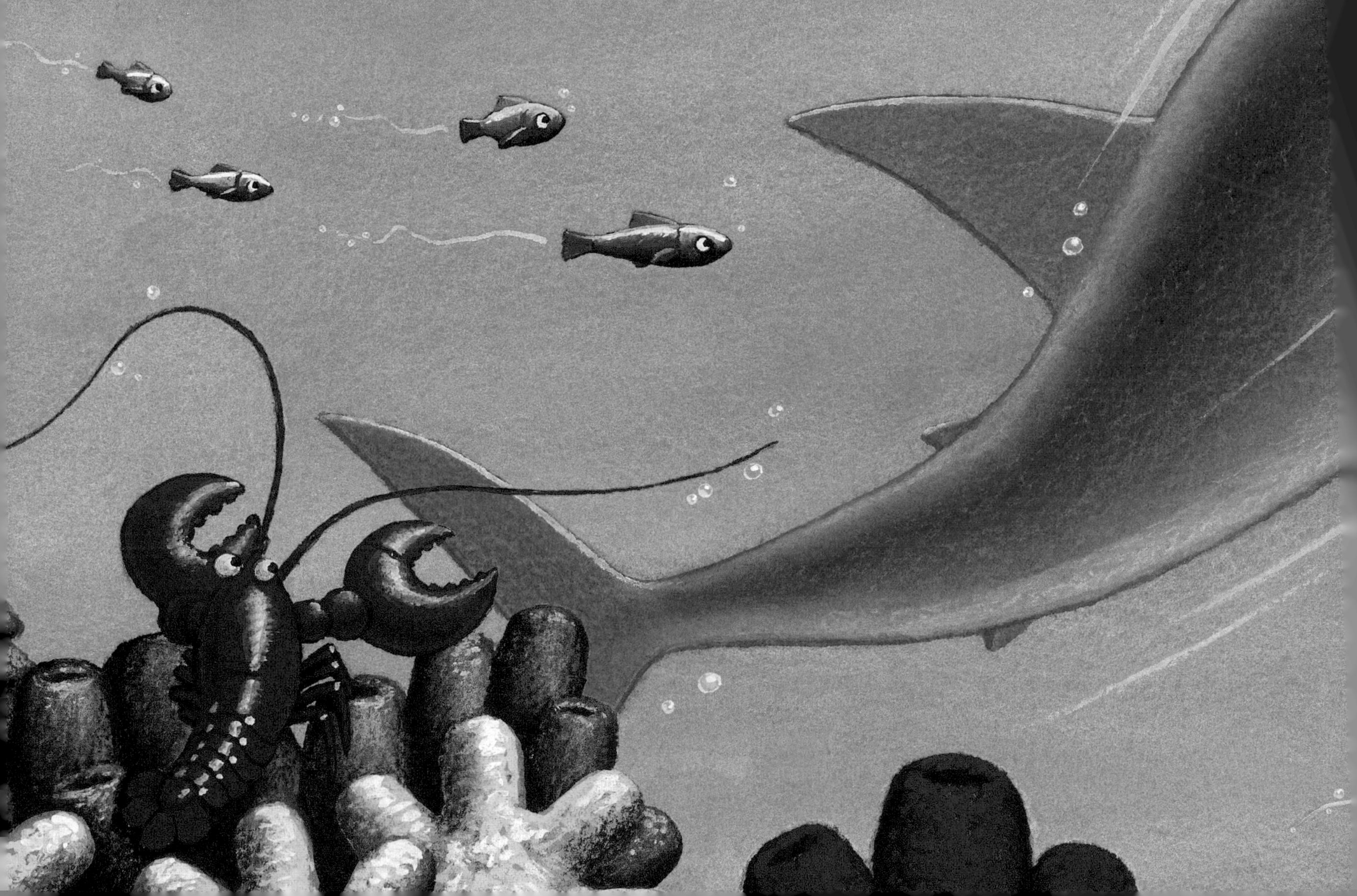

Then they swam off, **SERIOUSLY SCARY**, together.